Uncle Rain Cloud

by
Tony Johnston

Illustrated by
Fabricio VandenBroeck

TALEWINDS
A Charlesbridge Imprint

A TALEWINDS Book
Published by Charlesbridge Publishing
85 Main Street, Watertown, MA 02472
(617) 926-0329
www.charlesbridge.com

Library of Congress Cataloging-in-Publication Data
Johnston, Tony.
   Uncle rain cloud/Tony Johnston; illustrated by
Fabricio VandenBroeck.
      p.   cm.
   "A Talewinds book."
   Summary: Carlos tries to help his uncle, who is
frustrated and angry at his inability to speak English,
adjust to their new home in Los Angeles.
   ISBN 0-88106-371-1 (reinforced for library use)
[1. Uncles—Fiction. 2. English language—Fiction.
3. Mexican Americans—Fiction.] I. VandenBroeck,
Fabricio, 1954- ill. II. Title.
PZ7.J6478   Un 2000
[E]—dc21   99-054195

Printed in South Korea
(hc) 10 9 8 7 6 5 4 3 2 1

Illustrations done in acrylics and colored pencils
on hand-textured paper.
Display type and text type set in Burweed and Veljovik
Color separations made by Eastern Rainbow,
Derry, New Hampshire
Printed and bound by Sung In Printing, South Korea
Production supervision by Brian G. Walker
Designed by Diane M. Earley

For all the "little translators,"
especially Kiovanna Rodriguez

And for my favorite Mexican
tongue-twister town,
Parangaricutirimícuaro, Michoacán

—T. J.

For Jacqueline, Nadia, Carlo,
Fabio, and Alexis

—F. V. B.

"Tío Tomás looks like a black cloud about to rain." That's what Carlos thought when he saw his uncle waiting for him after school. He'd looked grim ever since the family'd moved to LA.

"*La única cosa buena de Los Angeles es su nombre,*" he always said. Like being named for angels was LA's one good claim.

He was a total cloud of gloom. "Uncle Rain Cloud," muttered Carlos. "The perfect name for him."

Uncle Tomás looked darkest on shopping day.
Like today.

Carlos's parents always left for work before
sunrise, what Mamá called "the first braids of light."
Tía Sofía used to shop. She was so fussy about it,
the family called her *La Jefa*, the boss-lady of the
market. But now she was sick. She stayed mostly
in bed doing small jobs, like mending, for Mamá.
Uncle Tomás and Carlos went shopping instead.

"*Hola, Tío,*" Carlos called.

Uncle Tomás greeted him with a grunt.
"*Vámonos.*" His voice sounded stormy. Not real
anxious to go.

The market was crowded with carts. Like cars jammed up on the freeway. Slowly, Carlos and his uncle inched along. Uncle Tomás didn't read English, so he studied the pictures on cans and stuff.

"*Te ayudo, Tío?*" Carlos asked.

"*No necesito ayuda*," he snapped. He never needed help.

Uncle Tomás fumed at everything they selected. "Milk." "Apples." "Eggs." He spat out the few words he knew like chewed fingernails. To him they sounded ugly— like all of "el Blah-Blah," English. But when they passed the tortillas, Uncle Tomás grabbed some and poked the word on the label.

"*Tortillas siempre son tortillas.*"

Carlos thought, "Tortillas always are tortillas—at least *something's* right."

No matter how grouchy by day, at night, like a worn-out storm, Tío Tomás grew a little calm. While Mamá and Papá shared their day's trials, he told Carlos stories of Mexico, tales of the tongue-twister gods, *los dioses trabalenguas*— *Tezcatlipoca*, Smoking Mirror; *Huitzilopochtli*, Left-Handed Hummingbird; *Coyolxauhqui*, She with Golden Bells; *Chalchiuhtotolín*, Precious Turkey, also called *Yoalli Ehécatl*, the Wind.

The harder the names, the more
Carlos liked to say them. Sometimes he
and Uncle Tomás tried to see how fast
they could reel them off. Their tongues
stumbled. Bumblers in the dark. They
laughed when they got jumbled up.

Carlos loved his uncle's stories. He wanted to know all about long-ago Mexico, when the people spoke to Corn. They called it Your Lordship, for without it they could not live.

In the market, when he passed the corn, Carlos said, "Hi, Your Lordship." And he bowed.

When it was time for Carlos's teacher conference, his parents could not go. To gain strength, Tía Sofía must still rest a lot. So who went? Tío Tomás.

For pride, he insisted they bring a gift.

"*Una manzana. Muy gringo,*" he grumped, plunking the apple down like a red rock. Carlos could almost see Tío's anger, perched darkly on his shoulder. Uncle Tomás might wish to be polite, but his weak English made him flare.

"Hello," the teacher greeted them, unflustered. Uncle Tomás muttered something, but it wasn't "hello." Storm alert—again.

"Please, Uncle Rain Cloud," Carlos said inside himself, "don't get all mad at English now." He prayed to be invisible. Like a little green *gusano* coiled inside an apple. No luck. Still there, about as hidden as his chair.

"I'm very pleased with Carlos's work," his teacher said.

"My uncle doesn't speak English," Carlos whispered miserably.

He knew Uncle Tomás would really blow at that. And he did. Like a silent hurricane, he glared at all things in his path, as if he hoped to flatten them with anger—the chalkboard, the desks, and, of course, those *malditos* books, all in English.

"Then you translate for us." The teacher smiled at Carlos.

She asked Uncle Tomás questions. Gripping his chair, Carlos explained. Back and forth. Forth and back the words lurched. Like a thirsty man lugging well water.

Once the teacher joked, "Are you telling your uncle *everything* I say about your work?"

"*Almost* everything."

Carlos and his teacher laughed. Uncle Rain Cloud scowled.

Later he grilled Carlos about what she'd said.

"*Qué chistoso*," said his uncle sourly. To him, nothing was funny.

That night Carlos wanted a story. About *Temazcaltoci*, Grandmother of the Baths. No, that might remind Tío of something Carlos would rather skip. Better to hear how the huge stone *Tláloc* got trucked from its old home to Mexico City. How its anger brought a furious storm.

So Carlos begged, "*Tío, cuénteme el cuento del Tláloc y el aguacerazo.*"

"*No! Sólo te gusta el inglés!*" Uncle Tomás yelled, like English was some bad disease.

Carlos looked at his uncle. Tears brimmed his eyes.

It was quiet a long time. Then Uncle Tomás began fumbling. Gently. In Spanish. Carefully, he placed his fingertips together, forming a ball of air, as if that helped him put his words together.

"Carlitos . . . forgive me. These days I am not myself. My *maldito* pride—I feel like a broken-winged bird. A thing that just flops around. You speak for me, a grown man, because—" he said, opening his big hands once more, "because I am . . . afraid to speak English."

Carlos sat stunned. A man and a boy, feeling the same! How could that be?

"It's like that with me, too," he said slowly. "Every day at school, I'm a little afraid. Sometimes it's rough. Kids tease me about my 'lousy Eeengleesh.' But I must go, I must speak. And now I've got friends. I can do stuff. English is pretty OK."

Uncle Tomás put an arm around Carlos. He sat silent, then at last said, "One finds courage in many places. Even in the third grade."

In bed, Carlos closed his eyes
and listened deeply to the night.
Once he thought he heard
something—something flapping. . . .

Shopping days were good after that. When Uncle Tomás and Carlos poked up and down the market aisles, Carlos pointed to things and named them. Tío Tomás said them back, stretching the words out clear to Mexico.

"Potato."

"Po-taaaaay-to."

"Cheese."

"Cheeeeese."

"Green beans."

"Greeeeen beeeeeans."

Whenever they passed the corn, they said, "Hi, Your Lordship," and both bowed low. If other shoppers stared, they got the same treatment—booming "Hi's" and sweeping bows to the floor.

One evening when they lugged their groceries inside, Mamá and Papá still weren't home. Another quiet night. Quiet except for Tía Sofía's snoring.

"Would you listen to that woman rumble!" exclaimed Uncle Tomás. "Like she was a big thunder swarm!" Then he told Carlos another rain-god tale, grumbling deep Sofía-rumbles for effect.

All that storm talk reminded Carlos of something.

"Know what I called you when you were always grouchy?"

"What does this 'groochy' mean?" Uncle Tomás asked, all innocent as milk.

"*Enojón*," Carlos said. "You looked like a cloud about to burst, so I called you Uncle Rain Cloud."

"You had someone else stuck in your mixed-up mind." His uncle chuckled. "*Siempre* I have been Señor Sweet-and-Kind." Then he added, "What is it you name me *now?*"

"I'm still deciding."

Uncle Tomás grinned. "No problem. Call me Your Lordship," he suggested. "Just like Mr. Corn."

They hugged each other hard, and they could feel each other laughing.

Then Uncle Tomás slipped back into Spanish, as he did for important things.

"You have taught me much English, Carlitos. I no longer feel like a broken bird." He flapped his bony elbows like awkward wings. "We will make a deal. You keep teaching me 'el Blah-Blah,' and I will keep teaching you tales of your ancestors—and of all the tongue-twister gods. *In Spanish*."

Carlos's eyes sparked. He tucked his
thumbs under his armpits and strutted.
"*¡Claro!*" he shouted. "Of course! Then
we'll know twice as much as everyone else!"

A guide to pronouncing the names of the tongue-twister gods:

Pronounce these syllables as you would expect to in English.
Emphasize the syllable in capital letters. All "a's" are soft: "ah."

Chalchiuhtotolin: Chal - chee - oo - toe - TOE - leen

Coyolxauhqui: Ko - yol - SHAU - kee

Huitzilopochtli: Wheet - zee - loe - POACH - tlee

Temazcaltoci: Te - mahz - cal - TOE - see

Tezcatlipoca: Tes - ka - tlee - POE - ka

Tla'-loc: TLA - loak

Yoalli Ehécatl: Yo - AH - lee EH - cahtl (The "tl" here is not pronounced "tul" or like the "tle" in "bottle." Form the "t" with the tongue, and voice the "l" at the same time, around the tongue. Try it!)

Thanks to Fabricio VandenBroeck, John Frederick Schwaller of the University of Montana, and Tom Frederiksen of the Mexico Student Teacher Resource Center for their help.

For more information, visit the Nahuatl Home Page at
http://www.umt.edu/history/NAHUATL/
or Aztec Common Word Pronunciation at
http://northcoast.com/ ~ spdtom/a-res22.html.